hippopotamus

hippopotamus

h^un t

by Bernard Most

Harcourt Brace & Company

San Diego   New York   London

Requests for permission to make copies of any part of the work should be mailed to: Permissions Department, Harcourt Brace & Company, 6277 Sea Harbor Drive, Orlando, Florida 32887-6777.

Library of Congress Cataloging-in-Publication Data
Most, Bernard.
Hippopotamus hunt/Bernard Most. — 1st ed.
p.   cm.
Summary: Children on a word hunt romp through the jungle with a hippopotamus and find different words in the name of their animal companion.
ISBN 0-15-234520-5
[1. English language — Spelling — Fiction.
2. Hippopotamus—Fiction.] I. Title.
PZ7.M8544Hi   1994
[E] — dc20   93-39988

First edition

A B C D E

Printed in Singapore

The illustrations in this book were done in Pantone Tria markers on Bainbridge board 172, hot-press finish.
The display type was hand-lettered by the illustrator.
The text type was set in Antique Olive and Antique Olive Light by Thompson Type, San Diego, California.
Color separations were made by Bright Arts, Ltd., Singapore.
Printed and bound by Tien Wah Press, Singapore
Production supervision by Warren Wallerstein and Kent MacElwee
Designed by Lori J. McThomas

To all the wonderful teachers who play this find-a-word game with their students . . . Now find all the words that you can make with the letters of

APPRECIATION

More books by Bernard Most

How Big Were the Dinosaurs?
Can You Find It?
Where to Look for a Dinosaur
Zoodles
Happy Holidaysaurus!
Pets in Trumpets and Other Word-Play Riddles
A Dinosaur Named After Me
The Cow That Went OINK
The Littlest Dinosaurs
Dinosaur Cousins?
Whatever Happened to the Dinosaurs?
If the Dinosaurs Came Back
My Very Own Octopus

We are word hunters. We hunt for hidden words.

Come along with **us** on a "hippopotamus" hunt.

We found a hippopotamus with a very large **mouth**.

"Don't **shoot**," said the hippopotamus.
"Of course not," we said. "We are just hunting for words."

"**Oh**," said the hippopotamus. "You **must** let me help.
I know where you can find many, many words."

So we climbed on **top** of the hippopotamus.

The hippopotamus felt **smooth**.

We found a **map**. "Let's head **south**," suggested the hippopotamus.

We didn't find any elephants or monkeys or leopards.
But we found some **pups**.

"Here's one with a **spot**," said the hippopotamus.

We didn't find any parrots or snakes or lizards.
But we found lots of **hats**.

"Please **put** one on my head," begged the hippopotamus.

We found a camera, and we took some **photos**.

We were getting hungry. Luckily we found some **pots**.

We all had **hot soup**. Yummy!

We found a **hoop** around a **stump**. "We're on the right track," the hippopotamus said with a smile.

The hippopotamus tried **to hop** through . . .

. . . and landed with a **thump**. **Oops**!

"I landed in mud," said the hippopotamus. "I need a **push**."

We pushed the hippopotamus **out**.

We cleaned **it** with a **mop** and some **soap**.

"Could we please **sit**?" we asked. "We're getting tired."
"Bul we're almost there," said the hippopotamus.

"Look **up** in the sky," said the hippopotamus.
"Follow those **moths**."

We found a hidden **path**. "There are your missing animals,"
the hippopotamus said with a laugh.

We followed them into a very large **hut**.

"Here's where you can find the **most** words," said the hippopotamus proudly. "A library!"